Lars Klinting

REGAL

the Golden Eagle

Translated by Alan Bernstein

R&S
BOOKS

Stockholm   New York   Toronto   London   Adelaide

Far beyond the meadows and mountains,
there was a forest. Large and small animals
lived in the forest. Some had their homes
beneath the ground, others in the field and
some up in the trees. High above them all,
the golden eagles soared on mighty wings.
They loved to fly. All except . . .

. . . Regal. He was afraid of heights. When he tried to fly, he became dizzy and fainted. Secretly, though, Regal dreamed of soaring up among the clouds with the other eagles.

Sometimes he flew
through the bushes,

but mostly he perched
on his favorite tree stump

or took a walk.

One day, Regal sat watching a pair of eagles.
"How will I ever learn to fly like that?"
he asked himself.

"I might have an answer for you," said a small voice.
"What. Who's that?" Regal looked around.
"Here I am, right in front of you," said the voice.
"Who are you?" asked Regal.

"I'm the goldcrest, and perhaps I can teach you to fly."
"You?" Regal laughed. "You're smaller than my tiniest feather. How could you help me?"
"You'll see," said the goldcrest. "Meet me on the hill by the edge of the forest just after sunrise."

"No, nooo!" said Regal. "Not there. That's too high. I'll faint."

"Too bad," said the goldcrest. "Then I really can't help you."

"But . . ." stammered Regal. "Wait. Don't go." He thought hard. "All right," he said. "I'll try."

Early the next morning, Regal began the long climb up the hill. The higher he got, the worse he felt. Finally, he reached the top, sweaty, dizzy, and exhausted. He couldn't see the goldcrest anywhere.

I've been tricked, thought Regal. How will I ever get back down to my dear old forest now? All day long, he sat there, wishing he hadn't listened to the little bird.
By nightfall, he had begun to wonder what it would be like to live on the hill for the rest of his life. Then he heard a tiny voice. "I guess I'm a bit late."

"We'll begin tomorrow, instead. It's too dark now," said the goldcrest.

"I'll have to wait here," said Regal.

"No," said the goldcrest. "Tomorrow we'll meet on that tree stump."

Regal trembled. That was even farther up the hill.

"Never," he said. "That's too high."

"Too bad," said the goldcrest. "Then I can't help you."

Regal thought about all the eagles he had seen flying above the forest.

"I'll try," he said.

Early the next morning he began to climb the stump.

Backwards . . .

and forwards . . .

Finally, he reached the top. The goldcrest was nowhere in sight.
Tricked again, thought Regal. "How will I get down from the stump and then from the hill? He sat there fretting for the rest of the day. When night fell, he heard a tiny voice.
"I guess I'm a bit late."

"Let's begin tomorrow," said the goldcrest. "It's too dark
now."

"I'll wait here," said Regal.

"Oh, no," said the goldcrest. "Tomorrow we'll meet in that
pine tree."

"The PINE TREE! I can't," said Regal. He was petrified.

"Too bad," said the goldcrest. "Then I can't help you."

"All right," said Regal. "I'll try."

And the next morning
he began to climb.

I'm going to faint, he thought.
But he didn't.
He sat perfectly still, afraid to move a feather.
Then he heard a tiny voice. "I'm so glad you could come."

"HELP ME!" begged Regal. "How am I ever going to get down from this horrible pine tree?"

"See that eagle up there?" said the goldcrest. "He could probably tell you."

"But how can I ask him? He's too far away."

"Fly," said the goldcrest.

"How?" asked Regal.
"Jump," said the goldcrest.
"Then stretch your wings."
"All right," said Regal.
He closed his eyes and . . .

jumped!

"More to the left,"
cried the goldcrest.
"A little higher. Good!
Now straight ahead."

Regal saw the forest far below him. If only that eagle can help me, he thought.

When he got close, he cleared his throat and said:
"Excuse me."

But at that moment he realized he was flying.
"There's no need to fly any higher," said the goldcrest.
"I'm flying," whispered Regal.

"What was it you wanted?" asked the other eagle.
But Regal didn't hear him . . .

He was already far away. Finally, he was flying high among the clouds like the other eagles. His wings felt strong, and he had a funny sensation in his stomach as he gazed at the countryside far beneath him. How good it was to feel the warm summer breeze lift him higher and higher.

ISBN 91 29 58774 3

Rabén & Sjögren Stockholm

Text and illustrations copyright © 1982 by Lars Klinting
Translation copyright © 1988 by Alan Bernstein
All rights reserved
Library of Congress catalog card number: 87-26595
Originally published in Sweden under the title *Örjan – den höjdrädda örnen*
by Rabén & Sjögren, 1982
Printed in Denmark 1988
First American edition, 1988
First published in the United Kingdom 1988

ISBN 91 29 58774 3

R&S Books are distributed in the United States of America by Farrar, Straus and Giroux, New York;
in the United Kingdom by Ragged Bears, Andover;
in Canada by Methuen Publications, Toronto, Ontario;
and in Australia by ERA Publications, Adelaide